Dear Parent:
Your child's love of reading s

Every child learns to read in a different way and at his or her own speed. Some go back and forth between reading levels and read favorite books again and again. Others read through each level in order. You can help your young reader improve and become more confident by encouraging his or her own interests and abilities. From books your child reads with you to the first books he or she reads alone, there are I Can Read Books for every stage of reading:

SHARED READING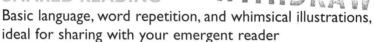
Basic language, word repetition, and whimsical illustrations, ideal for sharing with your emergent reader

BEGINNING READING
Short sentences, familiar words, and simple concepts for children eager to read on their own

READING WITH HELP
Engaging stories, longer sentences, and language play for developing readers

READING ALONE
Complex plots, challenging vocabulary, and high-interest topics for the independent reader

ADVANCED READING
Short paragraphs, chapters, and exciting themes for the perfect bridge to chapter books

I Can Read Books have introduced children to the joy of reading since 1957. Featuring award-winning authors and illustrators and a fabulous cast of beloved characters, I Can Read Books set the standard for beginning readers.

A lifetime of discovery begins with the magical words **"I Can Read!"**

Visit www.icanread.com for information
on enriching your child's reading experience.

I Can Read Book® is a trademark of HarperCollins Publishers.

Wonder Woman: I Am an Amazon Warrior
Copyright © 2017 DC Comics.
WONDER WOMAN and all related characters and elements © & ™ DC Comics.
(s17)

HARP38972
Printed in the United States of America. No part of this book may be used or reproduced in any manner whatsoever without written permission except in the case of brief quotations embodied in critical articles and reviews. For information address HarperCollins Children's Books, a division of HarperCollins Publishers, 195 Broadway, New York, NY 10007.
www.icanread.com

Library of Congress catalog card number: 2016963710
ISBN 978-0-06-268184-3

Book design by Erica De Chavez

17 18 19 20 21 LSCC 10 9 8 7 6 5 4 3 2 1
❖
First Edition

I Can Read!

READING 2 WITH HELP

WONDER WOMAN

I AM AN AMAZON WARRIOR

Adapted by Steve Korté

Illustrated by Lee Ferguson

Wonder Woman created by William Moulton Marston

HARPER

An Imprint of HarperCollinsPublishers

DIANA PRINCE / WONDER WOMAN

Born on the island of Themyscira, Diana is an Amazon princess. She trained with the other Amazons to become a warrior, and when she was ready, she joined our world to bring peace to mankind.

HIPPOLYTA

Hippolyta is queen of the Amazons and also Diana's mother. She is a skilled warrior, a wise ruler, and a loving mother.

ZEUS

Zeus is the king of the gods. He, along with other gods and goddesses, created the Amazons to bring peace to mankind.

ARES

The God of War, Ares loves war and conflict. He is an enemy to the Amazons.

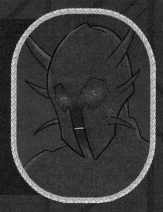

ANTIOPE

Antiope is the general of the Amazons, and trained Diana in the art of combat. She is also Queen Hippolyta's sister.

STEVE TREVOR

Steve Trevor is the first man to set foot on the island of Themyscira. He brought Diana to his world to help stop the war.

May I tell you a secret?

At a museum in France,

where I study ancient art,

I am known as Diana Prince.

But that is not my real name.

My real name is Diana,

princess of Themyscira.

I am an Amazon princess

from a faraway island.

Many years ago, I left my home
to protect the world.

When I did that, I took a new name.

That name is Wonder Woman.

My mother, Hippolyta,
is the queen of the Amazons.
When I was a child, she told me
how the Amazons came to be.

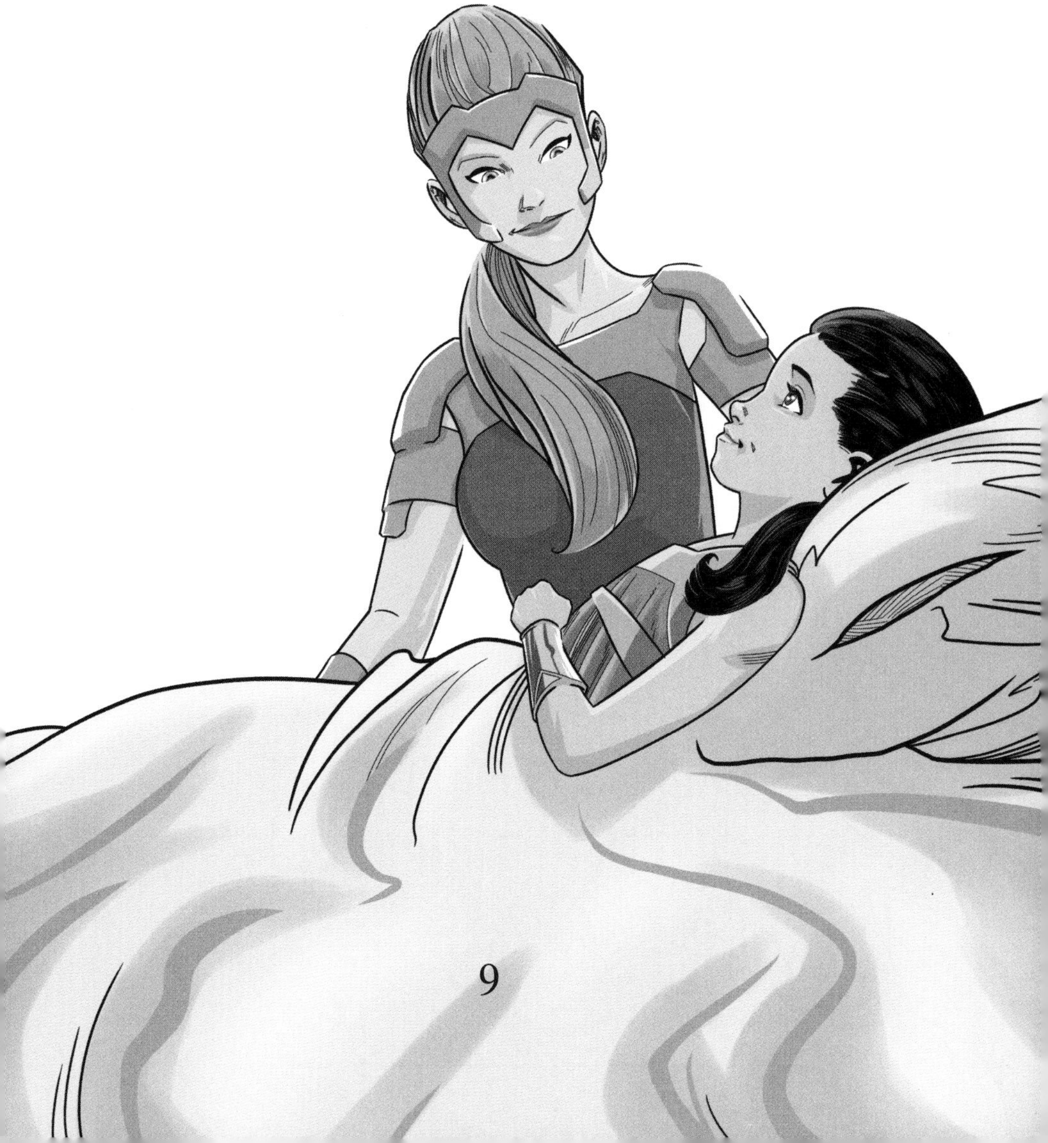

Many years ago, the Greek gods

ruled the world.

Zeus was the king of the gods.

He created a world

of peace and harmony for all.

But one god grew jealous

of Zeus's plan.

He was Ares, the God of War.

Ares encouraged the humans

to turn on each other.

Zeus and the other gods

created a race of wise women.

They were known as the Amazons.

They taught humans that peace

and love are stronger than violence.

But Ares refused to give up.

He attacked the gods

until Zeus was the only one left.

With his last breath, Zeus created

the secret island where

the Amazons would be safe.

Queen Hippolyta and the Amazons

lived there peacefully

for many years,

far away from the outside world.

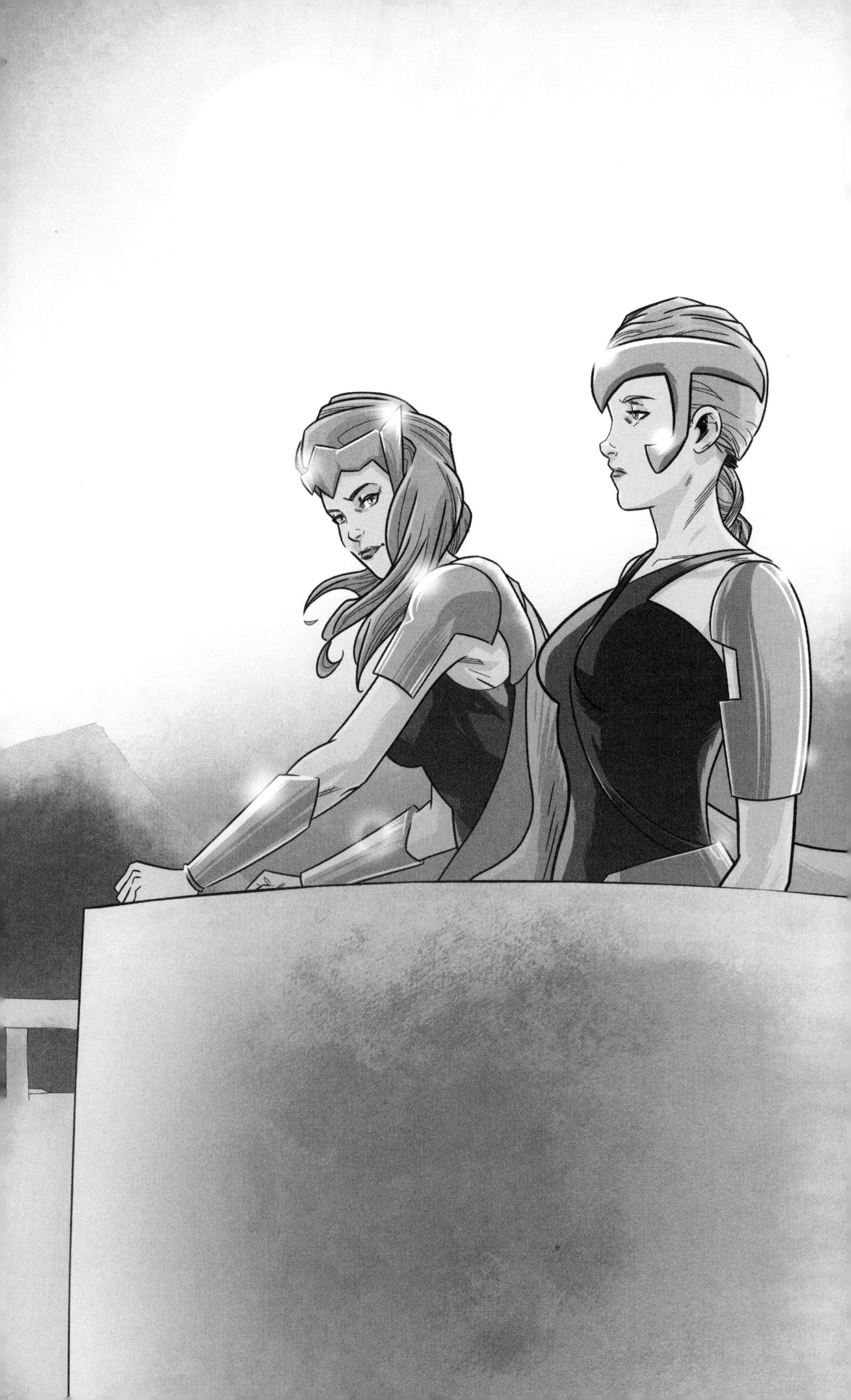

The Amazons trained every day.

They became very strong.

They hoped they would never

have to use their fighting skills,

but they knew Ares could return.

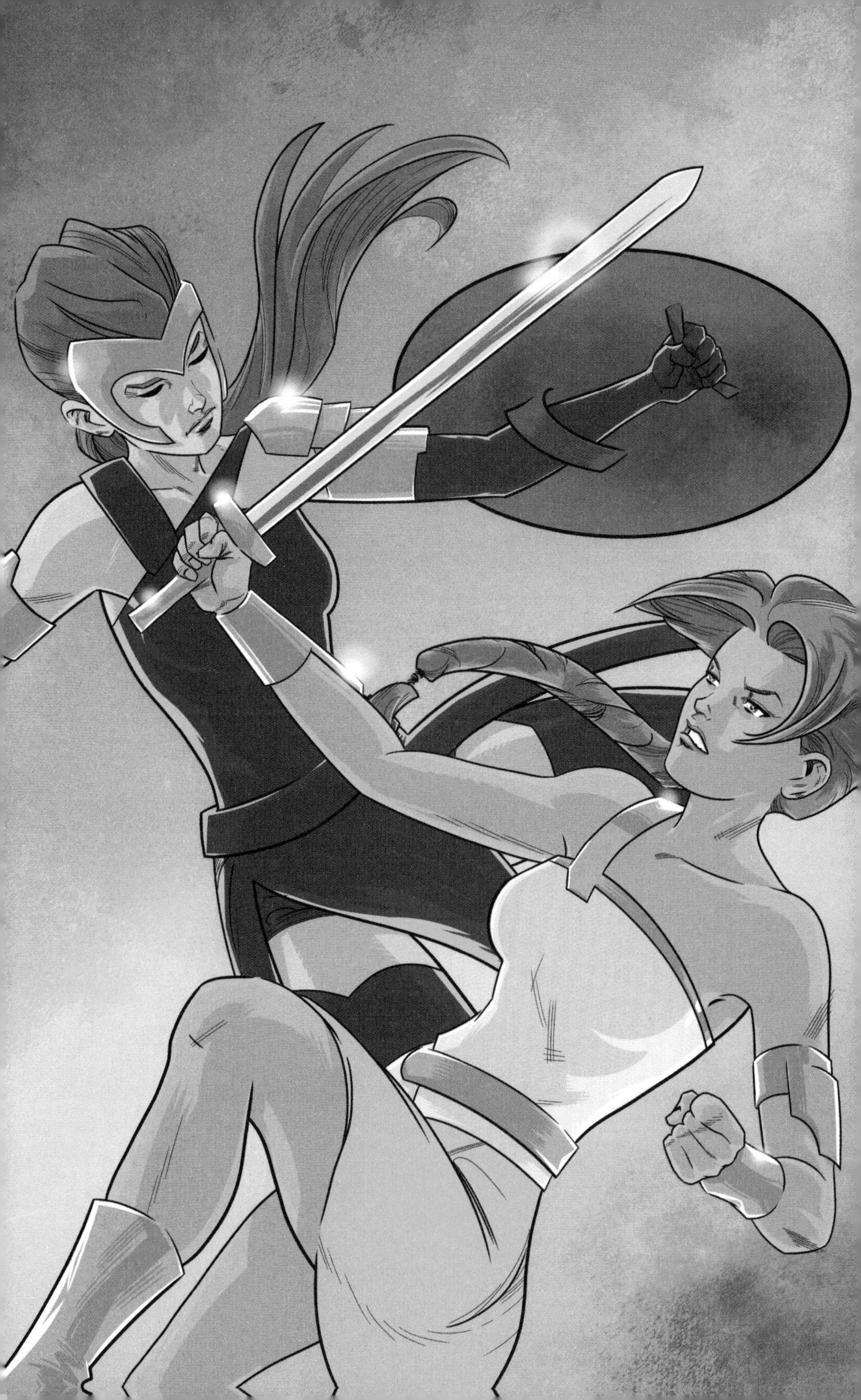

There were hundreds

of Amazons on the island,

but I was the only child.

Hippolyta had made me

from the clay on the island,

and the gods gave me life.

"I am going to name you Diana,"
my mother said, as I slept
peacefully in her arms.

Growing up, I was surrounded

by Amazon sisters and aunts.

I was their hope for peace.

They taught me about our world

and the gods and our mission

to bring peace to mankind.

But I wanted to train

with them in combat.

I wanted to be ready to fight.

My mother, our queen, said no.

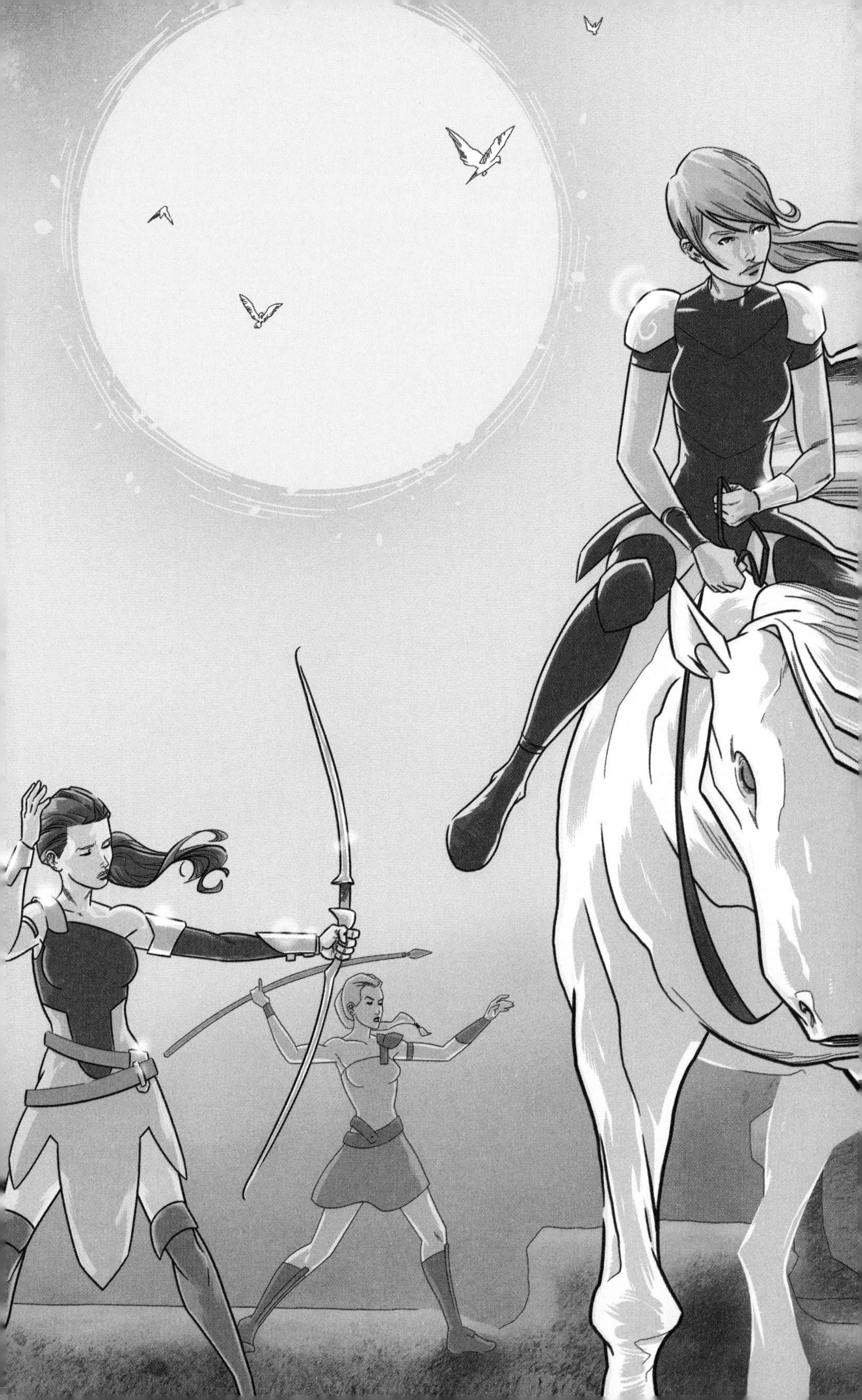

"Your mind is your
most powerful weapon,"
my mother told me.
I spent my time studying with
my tutor instead of training.

Antiope was the general
of the Amazons.

She knew I wanted to train.

She gave me lessons in secret.

My mother was unhappy,

but finally she agreed.

I worked hard,

and Antiope pushed me harder.

I wanted to be like

the Amazon warrior Artemis.

No one else on our island

was more skilled in combat.

Artemis was the fiercest

of the Amazons.

One day, I trained with

Antiope and Artemis together.

I managed to defeat both of them!

That day, a plane crashed

in the waters near our island.

It was flown by a man

named Steve Trevor.

He was an American soldier.

After I rescued him, he told me
that war was spreading
throughout his world.
I knew it was the duty
of the Amazons to try to stop it.

27

My mother didn't want to
put the Amazons at risk.
She forbade me to help,
but I decided to go with Steve
and fight in the war anyway.
I put on a suit of Amazon armor
and carried a powerful sword.
I also carried a golden lasso
that would force anyone
to tell the truth.

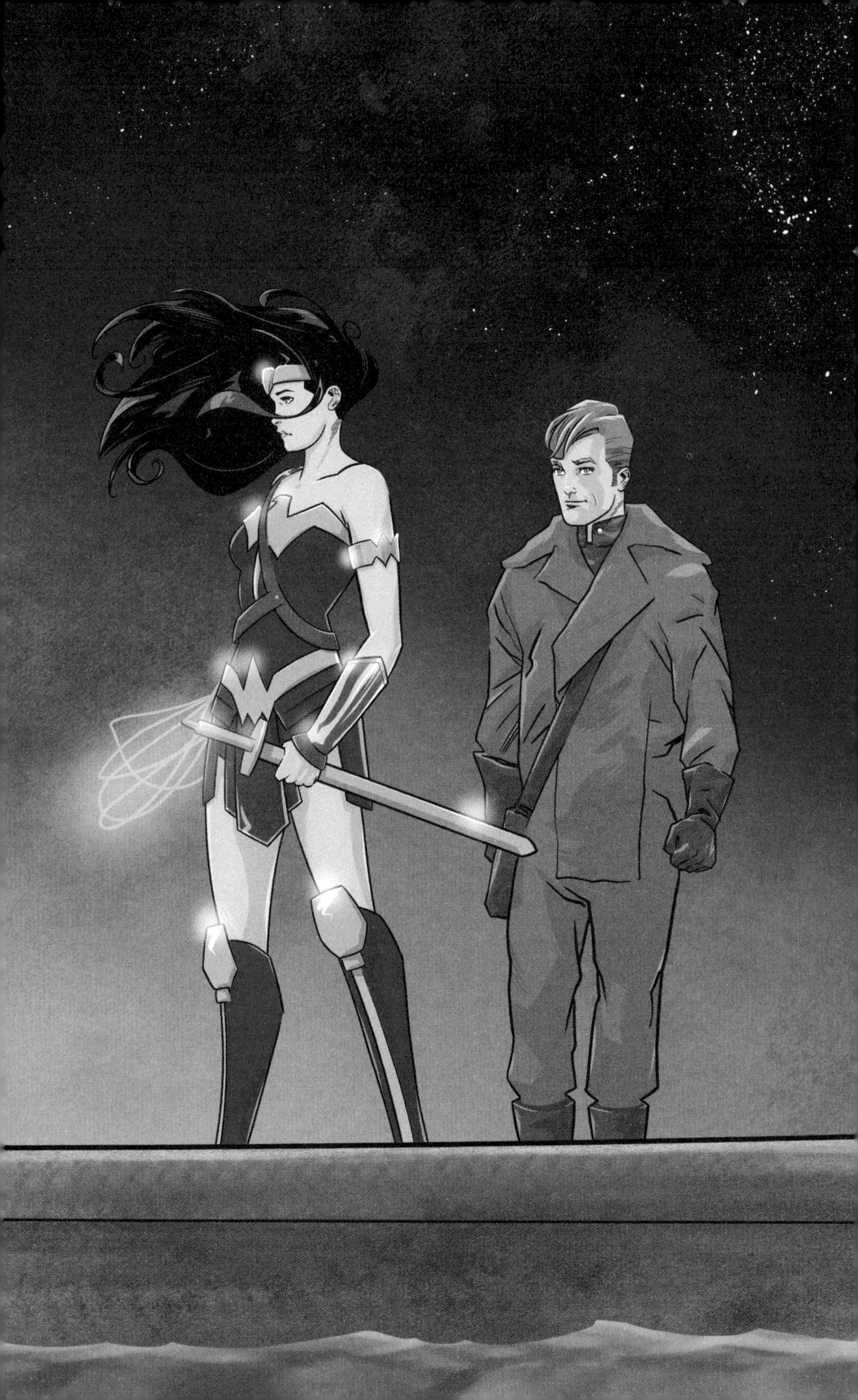

I said good-bye to my mother
on the shore of our island.
"I can't stand by while
innocent lives are lost," I said.
"I know," said my mother sadly.

As Steve and I sailed away
from my home,
I knew that a whole
new world awaited me.

This new world needed a hero.

I would use all of my training

with the Amazons

to make the world a better place.

I would become Wonder Woman.